IN THE NIGHT KITCHEN

MAURICE SENDAK

HARPER & ROW, PUBLISHERS

FOR SADIE AND PHILIP

AND THEY PUT THAT BATTER UP TO BAKE

A DELICIOUS MICKEY-CAKE.

BUT RIGHT IN THE MIDDLE
OF THE STEAMING
AND THE MAKING
AND THE SMELLING
AND THE BAKING
MICKEY POKED THROUGH
AND SAID:

SO HE SKIPPED FROM THE OVEN & INTO BREAD DOUGH
ALL READY TO RISE IN THE NIGHT KITCHEN.

WHEN THE BAKERS RAN UP
WITH A MEASURING CUP, HOWLING:

AND OVER THE TOP
OF THE MILKY WAY
IN THE NIGHT KITCHEN.

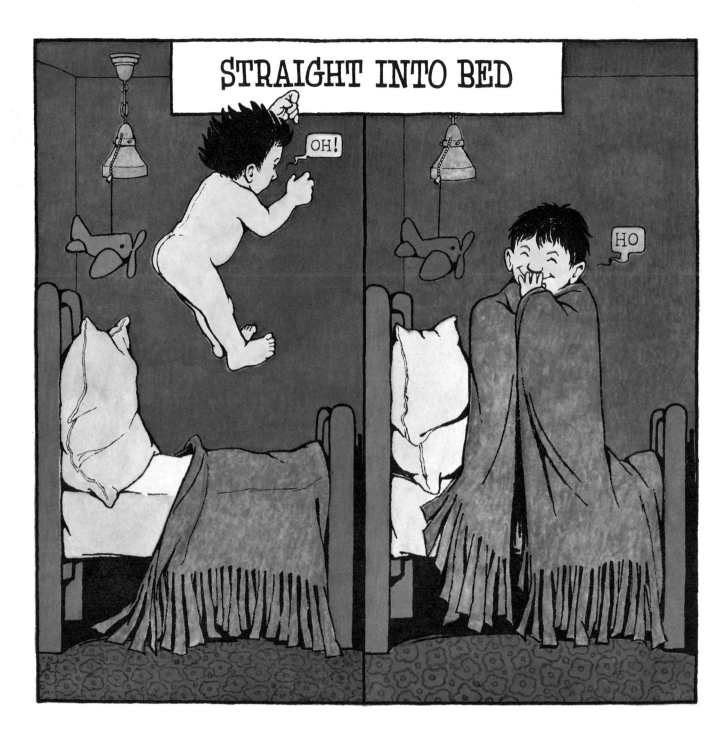